SHIELDING MONTANA

BROTHERHOOD PROTECTORS WORLD

KATE KINSLEY

Twisted Page Press LLC

BROTHERHOOD PROTECTORS

ORIGINAL SERIES BY ELLE JAMES

Hot SEAL Hawaiian Nights (SEALs in Paradise)

No plan survives first contact with the enemy.

Ryan

"I REALLY DO LOVE IT HERE," Montana whispers as we relax on the sunny California beach. Since the ranch is being taken care of, we both decided there was no rush to get back to Montana, and prolonged our unexpected stay.

I nod. "I do too. And I do believe Avery likes it," I chuckle. Avery is splashing Faith and Cade and is having the time of her life. "We know Faith's feelings about leaving here." Several thoughts have run through my head since we arrived in California. "What if we stayed?"

She furrows her brows. "What do you mean? I have the ranch—"

"We can sell the ranch." I move closer to her. "Cade and I have been talking, and we had an idea."

"Uh-oh," she giggles. "Should I be worried?"

"Momma, look!" Avery squeals as she runs through the water.

"I see you," Montana calls back. "Be careful!"

"I want to start my own security business, like Hank's, but here in California."

Her eyes move from Avery's to mine. "Really?"

I run my fingers through my hair. "Yeah. I spoke to Hank about it, you know, to get his blessing so to speak. He loves the idea."

A smile spreads across her face. "You want to help others like Faith."

I nod. Seeing how helpless she was, and the fact that if it wasn't for Hank, I would have never met Montana, I feel it's my calling. "I asked Cade if he wanted to be a vesting partner." I glance out at Cade, who has his arms around Faith.

"What did he say?" she demands.

I shrug, and she gives me a playful shove. Chuckling, I answer, "He's in."

"I never did like that ranch, anyway." Bringing

her knees to her chest, she asks, "So, what are you going to call your new security company?"

"Well, Cade and I have been bouncing around some ideas, and we came up with Gloriam et Protege Alliance."

Tilting her head, she furrows her brows. "What does that mean?"

"To honor and protect."

She moves closer, pulling my head to hers and places a soft kiss on my lips. "I love it, and I love you."

This is it.

This is the perfect moment I've been waiting for.

Reaching into my pocket, I seize the small red box I've been holding for the past few days.

It's now or never, Kane.

Dropping to one knee, I gaze into her inquisitive eyes. It isn't until I grasp her right hand that she realizes my intentions. Her eyes begin to tear, and her free hand flies to cover her mouth. "Abigail Montana," I croon. "From the second we met, I knew you were the one - the one I wanted to spend my days thinking of. The one I would spend my nights dreaming about. The one who would laugh with me, and occasionally at me. You are the one I want to share my life with." I pull the ring out of my pocket. Letting go of her hand, I open the box. She gasps as she stares down at the sparkling diamond in front of her. "You are the best thing that has *ever* happened to me. Please do me the honor of marrying me."

She drops to her knees and traps the side of my face with her hands. A smile cuts through the tears that stream down her cheeks. "Yes," she whispers on a breath. "Yes, I'll marry you."

I jump up and take her with me. Lifting her high in the air, I spin her around in my arms. "She said yes!" I shout to Cade and Faith. As I place her down, little Avery comes running over.

"Mommy, my turn. I spin!" she cries, lifting her little arms in the air.

"You can have a turn," she insists. "After Ryan puts the ring on my finger."

Shit. How did I forget to give her the ring? I glance down at my hand and find I'm still gripping the box.

"Sorry," I mutter through a smile.

Removing the ring, I slide it down her finger. I place a kiss on the top of her hand and turn to Avery. "Avery," I ask as I squat to her level. "I asked your mommy to marry me. Is that okay with you?"

She smiles. "Will you spin me more?"

I nod. "Of course."

Humming, she thinks for a second, her tiny lips pursed. She looks up at me with those huge blue eyes and appears to weigh out her options. "Otay. You marry Mommy," she announces, then giggles. "Spin me!"

Six months later…

Ryan

I EXIT my new office and stroll to my truck. Opening a security business was more challenging than I expected, but worth the effort. I've managed to book three clients this week alone. I'll need to hire some more men – something to be discussed with my partner, Cade, tomorrow. Now, to go home and be with my two loves.

A short fifteen minutes later, I pull in the driveway and place the truck in park.

"Hey, babe," Abigail Montana announces as I enter the kitchen, tossing a cardboard moving box on the floor. "That was the last one. We are officially moved in." Moving across the room, I pull her into an embrace. "I must admit, Ryan Kane," she murmurs against my chest. "Moving to California was the best idea you've ever had."

"I think asking you to marry me was the best idea I ever had," I counter, placing a chaste kiss on the top of her head.

She glances down at the shining diamond on her finger. "Maybe," she ponders, her grin widening.

"Where's Avery?" I ask, looking around the kitchen. I've learned pretty quick that if you can't hear Avery, she's up to no good.

She grins like a Cheshire Cat. "Taking a nap." She moves toward the kitchen island and hops up. "We do need to christen the house," she suggests as she kicks off her shoes. "We could start in the kitchen."

My love wants to play.

Now she's talking.

I move toward her as she peels off her socks. Ripping my shirt over my head as I approach, I toss it on the floor behind me. I'm not wasting any time getting us naked.

She wraps her legs around me as I get near and pulls me close. I palm her ass and haul her body across the counter. She slides, the apex of her thighs crashing into my pelvis. My hands find the sides of her face, her pulse drumming beneath my fingers like a marching band at a stadium. Seizing the back of my head, she grips my short hair and presses her lips against mine. Not innocently, like a tease but hot, fiery, passionate and demanding. She lets out little whimpers of anticipation that spur me on.

I nibble Montana's earlobe first, with just the right hint of passion. She groans, her breath hitching as I clamp down on her skin. My exhales curls against the skin just beneath her ear as her hands skate along the back of my neck. I place soft, feather kisses down her neck to her collarbone, then come right back up to her waiting lips… her waiting, infectious kisses.

Her kisses are so powerful and raw, that I forget where I am at times.

She gasps for air and parts her lips, but before she can draw in oxygen, I bite her lower lip and drag it into my mouth. Taking her chin in my hand, I suck hard. A garbled moan vibrates in her throat, and my cock twitches from the sound.

God, I love that sound.

I release her, panting hard. "Strip," I demand, taking a step back.

Her eyes gleam with desire as she does as I command. She crosses her arms at the bottom seam of her shirt and pulls upward, then carelessly tosses it on the floor behind me. Reaching behind her, she unclasps her bra and slides the straps down her arms. With a shimmy, her yoga pants and thong glide down her legs and drop unceremoniously to the floor.

This beautiful woman – the woman I love and plan on marrying – now sits gloriously naked before me.

Excitement spirals through me – adrenaline flowing through my veins causing my entire body to buzz in anticipation. You would think this was our first time, but every time with her feels like the first. My cock strains against the fabric of my jeans… throbbing, yearning, begging me to set it free. I need to be deep inside her to ease the pain – the only cure for my pulsing dick.

As I move toward her once again, she reaches out, her arms circling my neck. She drags me to her and thrusts her tongue into my mouth. Biting the tip of my tongue, she pulls it slow and sucks on it, releasing a husky moan as she does.

I'm not sure how much more of this I can take before I blow.

Using my neck as leverage, she swings her body off the counter and drops to her knees. With a flick of her fingers, my cock springs to life and before I can react, it's in between her lips.

A loud groan escapes my throat, the feeling exquisite. She moves her tongue around my shaft as she sucks, occasionally swiping it across the tip. When she does, I see stars. Painful desire tenses every muscle in my body. It's like electricity's shooting through my extremities. I slide my hands into her hair and guide her head as she works my cock.

Jerking my hips, I fuck her mouth, going deeper and deeper down her throat. I moan when she takes it all in, the head of my pulsating erection touching the back of her throat. Each time a spike of pleasure rocks through my body, I pull on the fistfuls of hair in my grasp.

She gazes up at me, her eyes on fire.

The way she possesses me... fuck, nothing feels better.

My grip tightens as I grow closer, but I don't want to come in her mouth.

I want her pussy clamping around me as she comes hard and loud... but not yet.

I pry her lips from around my cock and bend down. Placing my hands underneath her armpits, I haul her up and toss her back on the counter. Her brows furrow as she tilts her head, but she doesn't say a word. Grabbing the back of her head, I kiss her hard and fast. I force her mouth open, giving her no choice but to accept my greedy tongue. I kiss her fervently, sucking as much oxygen from her lungs as I can. My need begins to spiral, but there's something I have to do first.

Pushing her down so she's lying flat, I grip her from behind the knees and scoot her across the granite countertop so the apex of her thighs is hanging off the edge.

I kneel down and spread her legs wide, placing her feet on my shoulders. A guttural moan comes from deep within my throat as her perfect pussy is on display just for me. Montana closes her eyes as I skim the inside of her right thigh with the tips of my fingers, then find her dripping wet slit. I slide up to her clit and gently move my finger in a circular motion. She bites her lower lip in an attempt to stay quiet, but she can't. Without warning, I trade my finger for my tongue and she gasps, gripping the edge of the countertop. I grin inwardly as I suck the little nub between my teeth. She moans louder, her back arching off the cold stone from the pleasurable intrusion.

I work my mouth while simultaneously sinking a finger into her, slow and deep. Her feet press against my shoulders as she struggles to stay in control. She whimpers with each flick of my tongue, which only spurs me on. Her legs begin to tremble and spasm and I know she's close. I thrust my tongue in and out as I stimulate her clit with my middle finger. Her thighs vibrate as she clenches around my tongue, every muscle in her body shaking. She squeals as a rippling orgasm consumes her – spasming under me like she's being electrocuted, and nearly pushes me clear across the kitchen.

Wiping my mouth with the back of my hand, I crawl up her body. I crush my mouth to hers – an aggressive, no holds barred, take no prisoners kiss. Squeezing her breasts, I roll each nipple between my fingers. She expels a tortured moan – a moan I recognize.

"Please," she begs. "I need you inside me."

I begin to kiss my way back down. "If you insist."

Repositioning myself, I place her calves against my shoulders, her pussy wet and ready for me. I place the head of my cock at her entrance and slide in, slow at first.

"Ryan," she moans. Her eyes blaze with carnal need, so I pick up the pace. She groans as I continue my assault, and I grip her thighs for traction. I thrust in and out, over and over, not wanting the sensations to end.

She feels so tight.

So wet.

So euphoric.

Her muscles contracting and squeezing around my cock feel so amazing, they're driving the orgasm I'm trying so hard to control completely insane.

But I can't control it.

It's what she does to me.

Consumes me.

Every. Fucking. Time.

Losing all restraint, I slam into her, burying myself to the hilt. I slide my hands under her ass and angle her up. She clings to the countertop as I thrust my hips, submerging my cock over and over. "Is this what you wanted?" I growl through gritted teeth. "Tell me."

"Yes!" Her voice is nothing more than a strained whisper. "Oh, God. Yes!" She grinds against me, her walls beginning to tighten and contract.

She mewls – the sound is fucking magic to my ears. It's only a matter of seconds before she explodes, and I'll be right behind her. Her legs tense, and she begins to convulse. She tries to muffle her scream, but it's out of her control. My orgasm continues to build – trickling from the base of my skull down to the tip of my spine. Between the sounds of her losing control and her contracting pussy against my tender cock, my balls start to draw up. Once again, I see fucking stars and I'm sent soaring. My orgasm spreads throughout my entire body – every limb vibrating with pleasure as I grunt and go stiff, my cum spilling into her as I find my release.

Swinging her legs down, I collapse on top of her. I lay my head on her chest and attempt to breathe through the aftershocks that stroke my cock. This feeling... this feeling of complete and utter bliss leaves me in awe of this beautiful woman underneath me. The love of my life.

"Momma," a voice calls from down the hall.

For a second, I forgot where I was… and who could hear us. Montana sighs. "I need to clean up."

Placing a kiss in between her breasts, I disconnect myself from her. "No, baby," I answer as I pull up my jeans. "I'll get her."

CHAPTER 1

Abigail

As Ryan shuffles down the hall to retrieve my petulant four-year-old, I pick up my clothing that's scattered around the kitchen and scurry the opposite direction to the shower. Closing the door, I toss my clothes in the hamper and turn on the faucet.

Once the water is warm enough, I hop in. As I'm lathering myself, I think back to how something so bad could turn into something so wonderful. If it wasn't for my ex-husband almost killing Avery, I would have never met my knight in not-so-shiny armor.

The man who saved me in more ways than one.

The man who loves both me and Avery unconditionally.

The man I can't get enough of.

The way he makes me feel – it's euphoric. From his touch alone… God, I could spend all day naked in his arms. He's an amazing man from the tips of his toes to the top of his military haircut, and I don't know how I would have survived without him.

I turn off the water and dry off. Wrapping a towel around me, I exit the bathroom and follow the sound of singing. Upon entering the living room, I find both Avery and Ryan dancing to the baby shark song. Glancing over at me, he smiles and shrugs. Avery trots toward me.

"Momma! Do do do do do do!"

"I see, baby," I answer.

She keeps dancing, almost in place. It's adorable. "Sing wit us."

"Let Momma change first." I smile as she tugs on my towel, but I have a firm grip.

She frowns but recovers quickly. "Otay." Then she spins back to Ryan.

"Thanks," he mouths but grins through it. He may act as if he's bothered, but in reality, he loves it. She has him wrapped around her little pinky.

"I'll just be a few minutes," I inform him as I saunter to the bedroom, giving him a wink before closing the door behind me.

A few hours later, Ryan and I are heading to the caterer. We're lucky they have more than one location, since the lodge we're getting married at is over six hours away. My sister, Faith, and her new man and Ryan's partner, Cade, are watching Avery. She had them drawing unicorns before we even left the house.

This is one of the final steps before our wedding in a couple of weeks. I'm sure the food will be fantastic, but Ryan wants to make sure everything is perfect. Although this is my second marriage, I never had the fancy, over the top wedding. Ryan is insistent that I get my fairy tale happily ever after, and who am I to deny him.

It took forever for Danny, my ex-husband, to sign the divorce papers. Once he finally got it through his thick head that I was never going back to him, he conceded. Besides, he'll be in prison for the next thirty years, and once that reality sunk in, he knew there was no way of coming back from what he had done.

Do I feel sorry for him?

A little.

There used to be a decent man buried underneath the angry, bitter one. I'm not quite sure what happened to him.

Am I sorry he's in prison?

Absolutely not.

Trying to take my little girl from me... I will *never* forgive him for that.

One of the reasons Ryan's trying so hard to make this perfect is to try and take my mind off all of the negative things in my life – Danny being one of them. If he replaces this wedding with Danny's...

Ryan parks the car and we enter the restaurant. The banquet manager is waiting for us at the reservation desk. "Everything is all set. If you'll follow me, we'll get started."

Ryan and I trail behind the older gentleman to a small room in the back of the venue. One of the reasons we chose this caterer was the food, but it was the snow and scenic view from their Sierra

Nevada resort that ultimately grabbed my attention. I've always found winter weddings to be majestic, and this was the perfect option.

The next hour is spent tasting appetizers and different entrees, and by the time we've finished, I'm stuffed. It was a hard decision, but Ryan and I agreed on almost every single course. We give the gentleman our choices and get up to leave.

As we exit the caterer, my phone rings. I look down at the caller ID. Tanner. Why would Tanner be calling me? "Hello?" I squeak.

"Hey, Abby. Sorry to bother you, but I wouldn't call unless it was important." His tone is serious – that's never a good sign for a cop.

"No, it's fine," I mutter, confused. "What's wrong?" I hold up a finger to Ryan and take a seat on one of the benches at the edge of the building.

He sighs. "It's Danny." Silence stretches across the line for what feels like an eternity. "He's dead."

I gasp, my hand flying to my mouth. As much as I dislike my ex-husband, I would never want him dead. "Ohmigod! What happened?" Ryan sits down next to me, his brows furrowed in concern. I want him to hear this, so I put the phone down on my lap. "Ryan's here with me, you're on speaker."

"Hey, Ryan," he breathes. "Good, I'm glad he's

with you. He needs to hear this." He pauses a second, then continues. "They found Danny hanging in his cell. They're still trying to see if he committed suicide or if it was staged."

I close my gaping mouth. "That's awful," I whisper, still in shock.

"Good riddance," Ryan mutters. I glare at him, and he shrugs.

"There's more," Tanner groans, then sighs again. "Richard has completely lost his shit, and I'm worried about you."

It makes sense that Danny's father would be traumatized, but... "What does that have to do with me?" I blurt.

"He still blames you for his son's imprisonment. I fear he may seek retaliation."

Ryan bristles. "He'll never get near her as long as I have anything to say about it," he growls.

Tanner continues. "He's also bitter that you've moved out of state. Since Danny's dead, you have sole custody. Not that you didn't have it already, but if you're dead too..."

"Don't even finish that fucking statement," Ryan roars.

"He wants custody of Avery?" I squeak, my voice an octave higher than normal.

"That would be the only way for him to see his granddaughter," Tanner concludes.

Ryan stands, running his fingers through his hair. "Sonofabitch!"

"Just, be careful. If anything seems strange or out of place—"

"My head's on a swivel, regardless," Ryan huffs, cutting him off. "But I appreciate the warning."

"Alright, be safe," Tanner says, then the call disconnects.

I look at Ryan, who sits back down. Placing his arm around me, he pulls me close. "Don't worry. I won't let anyone harm you ever again."

CHAPTER 2

Ryan

SONOFABITCH.

Montana looks petrified, and I won't allow that asshole or his family to harm her ever again. The only thing we have going for us, is we're over thirteen hundred miles away from him and his money. He'll have to hire someone to come after us, and I'll be on the lookout.

Once we're home, I motion to Cade to follow me. As we go upstairs to the deck, I remove my cell from my back pocket. I need to speak to someone in Montana – someone local who can keep an eye out. My first and only thought was Hank. Right now, he's the only man I trust. Finding him in my contacts, I hit send and place the phone on speaker.

He answers on the second ring. "Ryan, how's California life treating you?"

I smile. "I love it here, weather is much warmer." I glance over the water as the sun begins to set. My eyes are fixed on the horizon, gazing at tangerine rays as they sink beneath the sea before twilight beckons the stars. I move to sit on one of the faux wicker couches Montana recently picked up.

One of the stipulations on moving to California was being close to the Naval Amphibious Base, the home of SEAL training in Coronado. The base was established in 1943 after the land was literally created from the dredging of San Diego Bay, done to allow large ships used in World War II to steam into Naval Station San Diego. It's also the only Naval amphibious base on the West Coast. Being this close allows me to recruit members to the GP Alliance more easily using the connections I gained from being a former SEAL. Originally, I was unsure of the house when Montana picked it but looking at the view from the second story deck…

"I bet," he chuckles. "How's wedding planning going?"

"Great. You and Sadie are still coming, right?"

"Wouldn't miss it," he replies. I can almost see his grin from here.

I stand and move toward the railing to look out at the darkening sea. As night deepens, random lights of fireflies blink more frequently until the canopy below sparks with benign, yellow embers under a star-speckled sky. Under normal circumstances, Montana and I would be relaxing on the terrace, transfixed on the beauty of the night – but I can't have her hear this conversation… at least, not yet. I run my fingers through my overgrown hair.

"I need a favor."

"Anything, you know that." His answer is quick.

The only man I trust in Montana.

I pace as I explain the situation as it was told to me. He listens, then speaks when I'm through.

"I'd heard he had gone mad." He pauses for a second, then continues. "I could see how he might cause a problem. I'll definitely keep an ear out and call you if anything flies onto my radar."

Pinching the bridge of my nose, I sit back down. "I appreciate any help you can give."

"Of course. I'll see you in a couple of weeks."

"Looking forward to it," I answer, then hang up the call.

I'm not entirely thrilled with his comment, "… could see how he might cause a problem." I don't know much about the man besides things Montana's told me. He's rich and always gets his way. Other than that, I know nothing.

Hank, however, knows him much better.

I turn to Cade, who heard the entire thing. "Thoughts?"

"He's got some set of balls if he thinks he'll ever have custody of Avery." He sits down next to me.

I nod. "I concur. Now, what to do about a potential situation?"

He shrugs his shoulders. "We need to hire more guys," he mutters. "Between the new clients, I'm not sure how much help I can be."

He's right. The two men we hired last month when we stated the GP Alliance are good, but we can only have one man to a client at a time. No. We need help.

"Reach out to Ethan and Mateo. Tell then we're working out of the house for the next week.

Let me see what I can do about getting us some help."

We go back downstairs. Faith and Montana are having a glass of wine while Avery is watching some cartoon. I move behind Montana and place my arms around her waist. Resting my chin on her shoulder, I ask, "What are you two lovely ladies up to?"

She turns her head so her lips brush against mine. "Up to no good, as usual," she quips. I nip her bottom lip, and she smiles.

Cade moves behind Faith, mirroring Montana and I. "We would expect nothing less," he chuckles, then places a kiss on Faith's neck.

"Why don't I put Avery to bed, then we can sit down and relax. Maybe put on a movie." Placing her hands on mine, she removes my fingers from around her hips, then saunters toward the living room.

A movie is a fantastic idea. Maybe a comedy. Something to get her mind off of Richard and Danny.

EARLY THE NEXT MORNING, I take the short drive

down Route 75 to NAB. My old SEAL commander, Michael Topper, is an instructor at the school. I'm hoping he'll be able to make some time to see me. I pull up to the guard booth and show him my credentials and tell him who I'm here to see. After making a quick phone call, he allows me to pass. I drive straight down Guadalcanal road toward his office. As I pull into a parking spot out front, he graces me with his presence.

"Irish! How the hell are you?" he calls out as he swaggers toward my truck.

"Good to see you, Top," I answer as I close my door.

After a brief embrace, he says, "Let's go talk in my office."

I follow him into a small building and down a long hallway. He opens the last door and ushers me in. "Thanks for seeing me on such short notice," I apologize. He hates last-minute plans, as most SEALs do.

"It's fine. Sit down," he answers, pointing to the chair on the other side of his monstrous desk.

I glance around – all of his awards and pictures with important people hang throughout the large space. Honestly, I never thought he'd leave the field. "How does it feel?" I ask, knowing I won't have to explain my question.

"Boring," he chuckles. "But it was the best thing for my girls." Michael has a wife and three girls, ranging in age from fifteen to five. "I see them more, and they don't have to worry if Daddy is coming home in a box." I nod. I get it, now that I have Montana and Avery. "How's your shoulder?"

I rub my right shoulder instinctively. "Manageable," I answer.

If it wasn't for Topper, I would probably be dead.

I was with him when the sniper bullet pierced through the car and into my shoulder.

It was Topper who was driving the Humvee and raced back to base before I bled out.

I owe him everything.

I turn my right hand palm up and attempt to wiggle my fingers. They move, but my range of motion is still compromised. Therapy helps – originally my range was less than half of my original capabilities. I still can't squeeze the trigger of a gun.

He shakes his head. "Yeah, that was a hell of a thing. Goddamn sniper came out of nowhere." He leans forward in his chair. "So, Hank tells me you've opened up your own security company." Hank and Top have known each other for years – and Top was how Hank got my number. I'm not surprised they've been chatting it up.

I owe him everything.

"Yeah," I answer, running my fingers through my hair. "That's why I'm here. I need your help."

"You know if I can help out in any way, I'll do it," he says deadpan. "Tell me. What can I do?"

I place my hands on my knees. "Can you think of any non-active special forces guys that would want to work for me? Abigail, my fiancée, needs me more now than ever and I have too many clients. I need a couple of more guys."

He smiles. Not a quick smile, but more like the Grinch right before Christmas. "How about Law and Order?"

My jaw drops.

They were part of SEAL team three – my team. "Seriously?" I ask, my brow furrowed.

He nods. "As serious as a heart attack."

Lawrence "Law" Grant was our foreign language expert from Mississippi. Wyatt "Order" Foster was our medic, who was also from Mississippi. The two became inseparable and were garnished the nickname "Law and Order." It's funny but very fitting.

"What happened? I thought both of those guys were lifers."

His face turns solemn. "Law's transport was struck by an IED, and he tore ligaments in his knee. Has a permanent limp now and officially retired a few weeks ago. Order came stateside when his mom got diagnosed with cancer and didn't have long to live. His tour was almost up anyway, so he chose not to reenlist but stay in Mississippi and help take care of her." Top pauses for a minute, then looks down at his desk. "His mom died last month."

Fuck. "Ah, man. That's horrible."

Top peers up. "If it means helping others, I know they'll both be in. Let me reach out and send them your way."

"That would be fantastic! I lost touch with everyone after..." After I got shot and essentially booted out of active duty and into early retirement, I was angry.

Really angry.

I cut off contact with anyone involved in the Navy.

I went and had myself a private pity party.

Then I got the call from Hank.

He helped me realize that I have just as much to give injured as I did when I was perfectly healthy.

He helped me relight the fire after I extinguished it.

Helped me understand that my team would still be there for me, even after I was injured.

I need to reach out to everyone and let them know I'm sorry for being a dick.

"You had your reasons," Top mutters. "Now, it's all about moving forward." He stands and I stand with him. Picking up a piece of paper from the desk, he walks around it to stand in front of me. "Irish, please let me know if I can be of any more assistance."

I smile and nod. "You've done more than I could ever thank you for."

He hands me the paper, then gives me a quick hug. "That's my cell. Call me anytime, brother."

I look down at the paper, then say, "I'm not working out of the office for the next few days until the wedding. I'll text you my address. Send Law and Order there."

"You got it."

With that, I turn and exit his office.

On the drive home, I can't help but smile. If

Lawrence and Wyatt do come and work for me, it'll be like old times. I trust these men implicitly, and they'd make a fantastic addition to the GP Alliance. I just hope by my radio silence, I haven't pissed them off too much.

As I enter the house, Montana is exiting. "I'll be right back," she announces. I turn and watch her try and steer Avery toward the car.

"I no go, Mama!" she squeals, trying to evade Montana's grasp.

"Where are you going?" I ask, my brows furrowed.

She side-steps left, grasping for the elusive child and misses. "She starts preschool today," she huffs as she lunges, and once again misses Avery by an inch.

It's like trying to lasso a cat.

Almost impossible to do.

Avery tries to run by me, but I manage to hook my arm around her waist and scoop her up. "Not so fast," I tease as I toss her over my shoulder. I saunter to the car with a squirming toddler hanging over my back. "You start school today."

"But Wyan, I want to stay," she whines, still struggling but starting to get tired.

Nearing the car, I place her down and squat next to her. "I heard they have snack time."

She looks at me, her blue eyes shining with curiosity. "What kind of snacks?"

"Oh, I don't know. The good kind," I answer with a wink.

She regards me for a moment, then shrugs. "Otay. Mama, I wanna go to skool."

Montana grins and shakes her head, then turns to pick up the tot. "To this day, I don't know how you do it," she mumbles as she places Avery in her car seat.

"It's magic," I tease and give her a gentle smack on the ass.

Closing the car door, she turns to me. "I won't be long," she insists, then places a chaste kiss on my lips.

As she gets in the car and begins to back out of the driveway, I can't shake this strange feeling that's suddenly come over me. I'm just glad the preschool is only a ten-minute drive up the road, or I'd be tempted to go with her.

CHAPTER 3

Abigail

AVERY'S HUMMING that stupid shark song as I drive her the short distance to her preschool. As stubborn as she is, I'm going to miss her around the house. Ryan keeps telling me it's only four hours a day a few days a week, but I'm not sure I'm ready for her to grow up.

Maybe after the wedding, Ryan and I should start discussing adding to our family.

He's an amazing father to Avery, and I would love to have a few more kids running around the house.

I pull in to the school parking lot and park. As I help Avery out of her car seat, the hair on the back of my neck bristles. I carry her toward the entrance, but after a few minutes, my neck begins to stiffen and tense – a tingling sensation begins to spread down my shoulders. Freezing in place, I glance around the full parking lot, but don't see anyone.

What the hell?

Why does it feel as if I'm being watched?

"Mama," she squeals. "I want snacks!"

I begin to move again. Trudging up the steps leading to the entrance, I insist, "Alright, Avery. We're here." I tug on the heavy glass door and we slide past. Shuffling down the hall, I find the office and check her in. A woman comes out of the back and is tasked the chore of escorting Avery to her classroom. "Give me a kiss," I whisper as I place her on the floor.

She places a wet kiss on my cheek. "Bye-bye," she sings, then spins to follow the woman.

After she disappears behind a classroom door, I turn and leave. As soon as I hit the bottom of the steps, that creepy feeling reappears. I can't explain how I know, but I just know that it's because of someone's gaze that my hair is standing on end.

I move faster to the car and just before I get in, I look up. Someone across the parking lot is looking right at me. Our eyes meet briefly, but I look away, slightly spooked. I feel way too uncomfortable to check again to see if the stranger is still staring, but my neck continues to tingle. Getting in the car, I slam the door shut, then hit the locks just in case my paranoia manifests into carjacking and kidnapping. Once the car is started, I back out of the space and slam on the gas. I need to put as much distance from this school and this disturbing individual as I can. As I turn the corner, I glance in my rearview mirror. The man is still standing next to a car, his head following the movements of my car.

The sensation feels almost paranormal — it's as if I can physically feel the eyes of that man boring into me, even after I've driven a safe distance away. I'm completely creeped out, and can't wait to get home to Ryan.

On the short drive home, every possible scenario runs through my head, but none of them make any sense. Why would some random stranger be staring at me? I've never seen him before in my life. He wasn't looking past me, either.

No.

He was staring right at me.

Right through me.

I pull into the driveway and turn off the car and wait – just to make sure the man didn't follow me. Once I'm satisfied, I exit the car and rush into the house. Ryan is sitting in the kitchen eating a sandwich when I enter.

I toss my purse on the counter and sit next to him. "I just had the strangest experience," I utter as I place my arms on the cool countertop.

Smiling, he leans in and places a kiss on my cheek. "I bet. Sending your daughter to preschool must have been strange." He takes another bite.

That was surreal, but not something I'd dwell over. Standing, I move to the other side of the island. "No. That's not it."

I'm not sure if it was my words or my tone that cause Ryan to lift his head from his plate. He takes one look at me and clenches his jaw. "What happened," he demands through his teeth.

I shrug. "I'm not entirely sure. There was this guy—"

"What guy?" he blurts, jumping from his chair and inadvertently causing me to jump as well. Placing his hands palms down on the granite, his face softens. He takes a breath, and as he releases asks, "Tell me what's got you so jumpy?"

I explain what I saw. He strokes his face as I describe the man, but doesn't say a word until I finish. "I'm sure it was nothing," he insists, moving around the island and placing his arms around my waist. "But if will make you happy, I'll pick up Avery after school."

"Maybe that's a good idea," I agree, melting into his arms. He leans down and kisses me. After just a few delicate touches of his warm lips, everything fades away and I become lost in the moment.

"Are you hungry," he murmurs in between kisses.

I am, but not for lunch. "I could be persuaded to nibble on something," I answer, then gently clamp down on his bottom lip.

He chuckles, his laugh vibrating through my teeth. Once I release him, he says, "I'm sure I can find something to whet your appetite."

THE NEXT MORNING, Ryan comes with me to drop off Avery and we go to finalize the flowers and photographer at the caterer. Once we're finished, we decide to have an impromptu lunch at the Calypso Café. One thing about moving to warmer California from chilly Montana is the ability to eat outside most of the year. And the views are to die for.

After we relax with our burgers and breezy water views, we head back to the house. Ryan is an observant driver, but he's being a bit extra today.

"Are you alright?" I ask as he switches lanes for the fifth time.

"Not sure," he answers, a bit hesitant. "I think we're being followed."

I spin to look behind me and search for what he's eluding to. "Which car?"

"The black sedan three cars back." His voice is eerily calm, and that worries me more than the lane changes.

"What are you thinking?" I can't stop looking behind me.

I turn to him and he shrugs. "Honestly, I'm not sure." He moves to the far-right lane. "Let's find out who you are," he mutters almost to himself then jerks the wheel, making a hard-right turn. Within a few seconds, Ryan is cursing under his breath.

"He still behind us?" I ask as I hold on for dear life.

"That's affirmative," he growls. I spin back around and see the vehicle coming up fast behind us, and the hairs on the nape of my neck begin to bristle. "What the fuck is this guy doing?" he demands, gripping the steering wheel harder.

The black car whips right and is now pulling up next to me. I glance over and my eyes grow wide. I try to warn Ryan, but the inside of my mouth lacks any moisture, and a croak was all that issues from my gape. I can't speak – all that comes out is a whisper.

"Ohmigod, that's him." The man in the black car rams his vehicle against ours, and I'm thrown against the car door.

Ryan regains control and makes the next left turn. "The guy in the parking lot?" he asks, again cool and collected.

"Yes." I breathe in and out, but air won't enter my lungs. Starved for air, my heart races at tremendous speeds – pounding so loud in my chest I can hear it. "What does he want?"

"I don't know, but I'm not sticking around to find out."

The black car tries to get beside us again, but

Ryan uses parked cars along the side streets as buffers.

"What are we gonna do?" I squeak, my limbs trembling in a way that has nothing to do with the motion of the car.

He turns right. "We're gonna lose this asshole."

Ryan keeps up his barrage of sharp, random turns, and finally the man in the black car gets stuck behind a bus and we lose him. Ryan keeps making turns until he's satisfied we're no longer being followed. Once he slows down, he reaches to the dash and hits the phone setting, finding Cade's name.

"Cade, it's me," he announces when Cade answers. "I need you to do a license plate search right now."

"Yeah, sure. Everything alright?" he asks, concern etched in his voice.

"No. Someone just tried to run us off the road, and it wasn't random." Ryan reaches over and grabs my hand. "I won't let anyone hurt you ever again." Bringing my arm toward him, he kisses the back of my wrist.

"Alright, go," Cade commands.

"California license plate, 5 Juliett Foxtrot Tango 732."

"Got it. Give me a sec," he announces, then goes silent.

I shift in my seat. "What do you think that man wants with me?" I muse.

Placing my hand back in my lap, Ryan strokes the back of my hand with his fingers. "I guess we'll find out."

"Ry, it comes back to an anonymous shell company. I'll need to do some digging to figure out who owns it."

"Fucking wonderful," he sighs.

I furrow my brows. "What does that mean?"

Cade answers. "An anonymous shell company is a corporate entity that's disguised its ownership in order to operate without scrutiny from law enforcement or the public."

"The people running a phantom firm don't want to be found and instead operate in the shadows—they don't have websites and create as short of a paper trail as possible," Ryan adds, shaking his head.

"Yup." Cade pauses, then says, "Once created, anonymous shell companies do little or no actual business. Instead, they often exist and function entirely on paper, opening bank accounts and owning assets without ever revealing the name of the true person benefiting from its conduct."

I frown. "How is that even legal?"

Ryan answers. "The company itself is legal, but sometimes people do illegal things and this is a good way to hide money from the government."

"Give me some time, and I'll have an answer," Cade informs us.

Ryan nods. "We'll be back to the house in ten minutes." With that, he hangs up.

CHAPTER 4

Ryan

THIS SMELLS LIKE RICHARD, and one way or the other I'll prove it. In the meantime, I need to keep my baby safe. I hightail it back to the house – at least I know she's safe there. I pull into the driveway and usher her in.

"I'll go and get Avery in a little bit. I need to talk to Cade and see what he's turned up." I give her a quick peck on the cheek and run upstairs to our makeshift office.

"Hey, Ry. I've got an update," Cade announces as I stride through the door.

I nod. "Good. I don't like this cloak and dagger shit."

I sit across from Cade, who's sitting behind my desk and typing furiously. "I made a few phone calls after I hung up with you, and it turns out the shell company is owned by another company called *Rexport*. I did a little more digging and found the company is based out of Eagle Rock."

"Motherfucker!" I stand and run my fingers through my hair. "That dirty motherfucker!"

"Who?" he asks, his brows furrowed.

I forgot – he's never met Richard or his asshole son. "Abigail's ex father-in-law, Richard. He lives in Eagle Rock."

Cade frowns. "He tried real hard to hide his identity, but I got friends in high places," he mutters as I pace around the room. The piece of shit doesn't want to get his hands dirty. "What do you wanna do?"

Good question.

What do I want to do?

I want to fly to Montana and place the barrel of a SIG Sauer against his temple.

I want to place my hands around his head and twist hard until I hear a snap.

But I can't do those things without fear of civilian repercussions.

So I need to think of a more legal approach.

"Let's do a little more recon and see if we can't prove beyond a shadow of a doubt that he's behind this. There has to be a money trail somewhere."

Cade smiles as he strokes his bottom lip. "That, my friend, is where I come in real handy. Let me go make some phone calls."

"Keep me posted. I'm gonna go check in on my girl," I advise him as I move toward the stairs.

I hop down the steps and find Abigail in the kitchen pouring a glass of wine. Her hand is shaking, and the fact that she's scared makes me really angry. I'll deal with this asshole one way or another.

"You alright?" I ask, even though I know the answer.

She takes a sip, then shakes her head. "Not really. I don't understand why some guy I've never seen was chasing us." She sits and sighs.

I promised myself I would be as transparent as I could be without compromising her safety, or causing her to have a panic attack. This is one of those times where I need to keep my musings to myself.

"I'm not sure," I answer, positioning myself behind her. Standing with my front to her back, I lean down and kiss the side of her neck. "But, I'm sure as hell gonna find out."

AN HOUR LATER, my phone rings. It's Law.

"Irish," he roars into the phone. "How the hell are ya, brother?" God, it's good to hear his southern twang.

"Never better," I answer. "I'm guessing you spoke to Top?" I pace around my office, nervous to have his answer.

"Yup. And whatever it is, both me and Order are in."

I sigh and take a seat at my desk. I knew I could count on those two. "Are you in California?"

"As luck would have it, yes. I'm in San Diego visiting my sister. Order's back in Mississippi, but he can be on a plane tomorrow."

Perfect. This could work. "Can you meet me later this evening? There're some details I want to go over with you and don't want to do it over the phone."

There's a short pause before he answers. "Yeah, I think so. You're in Coronado, right?"

"Yeah. Not too far from base. I'll text you the address. Can you be here by five?" It's just after three and San Diego is a stone throws away. That gives him plenty of time to get here.

"No problem. I'll see you in a bit." With that, he disconnects the call.

Perfect.

A FEW DAYS LATER, I wake Avery up early. It's Christmas Eve, and even though we're leaving for the Sierra Nevadas in a few days, I want to decorate the house. The fact that there's no snow on the ground will not deter me. I will make this house a winter wonderland.

"Hey, baby. Wanna come with me to surprise Mama with a Christmas tree?"

She jumps out of bed. "Can I pick the twee?"

I chuckle. "Of course, you can. Whatever you want." She makes a run for the door but I scoop her up before she can get far. "Not so fast," I tease as I toss her back on the bed. "You need to get dressed first."

I rummage through her closet and find an outfit that sort of matches. She puts it on without complaints, which I think is a first. I buckle her sandals onto her tiny feet and pick her back up.

"Shhhh," I say, placing my index finger over my mouth. "Mama is sleeping, and this is a surprise."

She giggles, then places her finger over her mouth. "Shhhh," she repeats. "I be quiet."

I tiptoe out of her bedroom into the kitchen. I scribble a note so Montana doesn't panic and make it out of the house without incident. Getting to the truck, I buckle Avery in and back out of the driveway slowly. Once I'm a safe distance from the house, I turn on the radio to that Disney station Avery likes, and sing along to some Mickey Mouse song she's always screaming. If it makes her happy, it makes me happy.

We wander around the tree lot for almost a half an hour before she finds a tree she likes. It's kinda big, but we have vaulted ceilings, so it'll fit. I pay the man and he attaches the large tree to the top of my cab with the trunk nestled in the back of the pickup. Now… to get ornaments.

Finding the closest Walmart, I carry Avery inside and plop her into a wagon. Abigail left everything in Montana, including all of her holiday decorations. She claims she wanted to start fresh, but with the wedding so close to the holidays, she never had time to go and purchase anything.

I push the tot to the back of the store and begin to sort through what's left of the decorations. I really should have thought of this sooner – the fact that we were going to be out of town shouldn't mean we can't decorate. She picks out brightly colored garland and some Disney ornaments while I try and find some more traditional decorations.

All in all, we wind up with enough to decorate the living room.

Now, to get everything into the house without Montana seeing it.

We leave the store and I stop and pick up breakfast for the starving child. She wanted French toast sticks, so I found a fast food place that sells them. Then we head home.

I turn the corner to pull into the driveway and find Montana standing on the front porch with her arms crossed.

Crap.

Busted.

I park and get Avery out of the car.

"Hi Mama," she squeals as she runs toward her. "We got you su-pize!"

As she picks up the toddler, she eyes the tree on the truck. She narrows her eyes, but it's through a smile. Shaking her head, she walks toward me. "Took Avery to breakfast, huh?"

I shrug. "I didn't lie. I fed her," I argue.

"You just failed to mention the other details," she quips, placing Avery down and peeking into the back seat.

As she pulls out a bag of decorations, I nod. "Well... it was early, and I was in a rush to get out of the house," I mutter in defense.

"Uh-huh." She picks up another bag and starts to walk back to the house. "Let's see how well you did, under the circumstances," she laughs, handing one of the bags to Avery.

"Let me get the tree, I'll be in in a minute," I call out as she opens the front door.

Untying the tree from the roof, I toss it over my shoulder and go into the house. I lean it against the wall and go back outside for the stand and whatever else Montana left in the backseat. Once I have everything inside, I begin to set up the mammoth tree.

"Was your goal to buy the biggest tree they had?" she asks as I assemble the stand.

I chuckle and begin to answer, but Avery beats me to it. "I pick the twee," she announces, jumping up and down. "It pitty and big!"

Montana gives me the side-eye as she praises Avery.

When the stand is assembled, I place the tree inside. Making sure it's straight, I move it toward the corner of the room so it's out of the way. I turn to retrieve the lights and find Montana standing in front of me with a mimosa extended outward.

"If we're going to decorate the tree, we need to do it right," she announces as she hands me the fluted glass. Moving closer she pulls me into an embrace, wrapping her free arm around me. "Thank you for doing this," she whispers close to my ear. Placing a gentle kiss on my cheek, she releases me and steps back to look at the tree. "It's perfect." Her smile is infectious, and I can't help but to smile back.

"You're perfect," I murmur as I hold my mimosa up. "Here's to us, and many more Christmases just like this."

CHAPTER 5

Abigail

I NEEDED THIS TODAY, and I don't know how Ryan knew it.

I needed some normalcy, and this was the perfect way to do it.

Between getting ready for the wedding and all of the other negative things going on this week… I've been a little stressed.

I thought about putting up a real tree but thought against it since we're leaving right after Christmas. I have some presents stashed upstairs that I still need to wrap, but figured I'd pick up a small fake tree sometime this week. But with the mystery man in the parking lot and then again trying to run us down... my mind has been elsewhere. I would have remembered later, and by then, I'm sure there would have been nothing left to buy.

I have something special for Ryan too, but I'll give that to him right before the wedding.

Sipping my mimosa, I can't help but smile. Ryan and Avery are making the perfect Hallmark moment as they decorate the tree. I don't want to interrupt their bonding moment, and I just sit back and soak it all in. She needs a positive male figure in her life, and I couldn't have chosen a better one if I'd tried.

There's nothing this man can't do.

He's an adoring soon-to-be stepfather, who treats Avery like she's his own.

He treats me like a queen, even though I'm not sure I deserve it.

He works his ass off to make sure we have everything we need and then some.

He's perfect, and I don't know where I'd be without him.

I make them stop for lunch and Avery's nap. Once she's awake, they continue to decorate the large room. Next year will be an expensive year to decorate this huge house, but I can't wait for it to really feel like home.

By the time they're completely finished, it's dinner time. I made Avery pasta with butter, while Ryan and I have linguini and clam sauce.

"Avery, are you ready for Santa to come tonight?" Ryan asks as she finishes her dinner.

Her face lights up. "Santa come tonight?"

I nod. "Were you a good girl this year?"

"Uh-huh!" she says with a smile.

"Well," Ryan continues, "good girls need to be in bed early, otherwise Santa will skip over the house."

Her eyes go wide. "Mama, I done. I go to bed now." She stands and presents me with her empty plate. Taking it from her, I place it on the table. "Come read to me," she commands as she tugs at my hand.

Ryan stands. "How about I read Twas the Night Before Christmas to you?"

My heart melts. That was something my father did when I was younger, and a cherished memory of my childhood. She moves to Ryan's side of the table and begins tugging on his fingers.

"C'mon Wyan!" she commands. He stands and Avery leads him toward the stairs.

"You need to brush your teeth first," I say as they begin to ascend.

I clean up the plates and wash the dishes, then head upstairs to see what's going on. I peek into Avery's room and see Ryan sitting on the side of the bed reading a hard copy of the book. He must have purchased it while he was out, since I no longer have a copy. But when I look closer, I realize it's not a new book. It's *my* book.

I've been an emotional mess all day today, and this just thrust me over the edge.

It's like a floodgate opens, and tears begin streaming down my face. Leaning on the door, I let the happiness soak right into my bones. I close my eyes and savor the moment – letting Ryan's words fall over me like a warm blanket.

After a moment, I open them again and watch as Avery is engrossed in the story. Her eyes are wide as she hangs on every word that leaves Ryan's lips. She smiles as she listens, and her joy is infectious. It starts as a tingle in my fingers and toes, much like the feeling I have when I'm anxious, but instead of worrisome, it's warm. It passes through me like a warm ocean wave, washing away all of my stress and leaving me refreshed inside.

Ryan finishes the story, then leans down to kiss Avery on the forehead. "Now, go to sleep, or Santa won't come. Understood?"

She yawns, then nods her head. "Goodnight, Wyan. Goodnight, Mama."

Ryan turns to see me in the doorway, then smiles. I use the back of my hand to wipe my tear-stained cheeks, then enter the room to tuck Avery in.

"I'll see you in the morning, peanut," I murmur as I kiss her nose.

She moves her teddy bear closer to her face and closes her eyes.

That's our cue to leave.

Once we're out of earshot, I stop and look at Ryan. "How?" It's the only word I can form as I stare down at my childhood book.

He dips his head forward, gently cupping his hair and smiles. "I may have called your parents and asked them if there was anything special you did around Christmastime. They sent me this." Ryan hands me the book. I stare down at it, still in shock that it's in my hands. The cover's faded and the pages are ragged and torn, but it's a piece of my childhood. This might be the sweetest thing anyone has ever done for me and Avery. He went above and beyond to make us happy.

I look back at him, and there's a softness in his eyes. His irises glisten in the dim light of the hallway. I move closer to him, our mouths pressing together in a long, passionate kiss. I draw my tongue over his teeth and swallow his groan of pleasure as we slide closer to each other, no visible gap between us. The taste of peppermint candy invade my senses – cool and warm at the same time.

I don't want this moment to end... this perfect moment.

He releases me, a wicked smile painted on his lips. "C'mon." Leading me down the stairs, he stops just short of the kitchen, then glances up. A sprig of mistletoe dangles from the entryway just over our heads. "Now, let's do that again."

He crushes his lips to mine, kissing me hard and deep. My desire for him surges through my body like a tornado, gathering speed and intensity. I don't think I could ever love or want him more than I do at this moment.

His mouth travels down to my neck and lands on my nape. Nipping gently, he begins the return journey. Using the scruff on his chin, he brushes it softly under my jaw. Bolts of pure lust move straight to my legs, and I'm barely able to stand.

When his lips find mine once again, I'm sent spiraling.

I need him.

God, I need him so badly.

Moving his lips from mine, they travel to my ear. "Dance with me."

Christmas songs have been playing in the background all afternoon, but I didn't pay any attention to a particular song until now. Nat King Cole's majestic voice croons over the speakers. Ryan drags me to the center of the living room and wraps his arms around me. We sway slowly – the sound of violins reverberating off the walls of the large room. I place my head on his chest and sigh. Resting his chin lightly on the top of my head, he holds me tight.

This.

This right here.

I couldn't have wished for a more perfect Christmas than this.

When the song ends, he takes my face in his palms. "Now," he murmurs as he places a gentle kiss upon my lips, "why don't we finish wrapping Avery's gifts, then take this party upstairs."

I smile. "I couldn't agree more."

AVERY IS up at the first sign of light and comes bounding into our bedroom. "Mama! Wyan! Santa came!"

I untangle my limbs from around Ryan and stretch my arms over my head. Ryan flips back the covers and stands, then throws a t-shirt over his head.

"Take your time, babe. I'll go make coffee," he orders as he takes Avery's hand. "Lots and lots of coffee." He smiles, and it's infectious.

"C'mon Wyan!" she demands as she tugs him out of the bedroom. His lips twist upward before he shrugs, then they disappear down the hallway. I laugh, knowing how much Ryan loves this time with Avery.

Aware of how impatient she can be, I throw my legs off the bed and stand, then shuffle to the bathroom. Avery's voice echoes off the walls before I can finish, and I don't have long before she has a meltdown.

I finish up and rush down the stairs. An awaiting mug of coffee awaits me as I hit the bottom, and we hurry into the living room. Avery is standing in the middle of the room staring at the tree, her eyes wide. My eyes move from Avery to Ryan, who's shoulder is now leaning against the doorway. The pile of presents grew from the time I placed them under the tree, to now. If I had to guess – more than double in size. I narrow my eyes at him, but his face remains stoic.

"Wow, Avery," he murmurs without taking his eyes off me. "Look at all of the presents Santa left you."

She sits on the floor in front of the pile of gifts, her legs bouncing up and down. "Mama, can I open?"

Still glaring at Ryan, I shuffle to the couch. I'm too tired to argue with him. "Sure, baby. Bring me a gift and I'll see if it's yours."

Avery finds the biggest box under the tree and pushes it toward my feet. I sure as hell didn't buy this one, but when I glance over at Ryan, he remains reticent. A smile does try to crack through his façade, but he doesn't allow it.

Bastard.

Leaning over, I read the tag. "To Avery, love Santa."

"Okay, Avery. You can open this one."

Avery pounces on the box like a lion on a gazelle, and she rips through the paper in record time. "A bicycle!" she squeals. "I like pink bicycle!"

"I'll put it together later," Ryan says through a smile. Laughing, I shake my head. This child has him wrapped around her little finger, and it's adorable to watch.

"More!" she shrieks.

Ryan moves to sit next to Avery. "Here, let me help you," he says as he reaches under the tree. Retrieving a medium size box, he hands it to Avery. As she's tearing through the paper, he hands me a small box. I furrow my brow as he places it in my hand. "I thought you'd appreciate this," he says with a shrug.

I pull at the red bow and unwrap a small black box. Inside is a small gold bar attached to a chain. Avery's name is written in script across the rectangle.

"Flip it over," he urges.

I turn it over and gasp. Her tiny fingerprint is pressed into the gold. "When?" I whisper, still in shock.

"I had Faith take her to the jeweler while we were out one day." I remove the chain from the box and undo the clasp. "Let me," he insists, taking the necklace from me.

Moving my hair, I turn my head to give him easier access to the clasp. He places the necklace around my neck, then kisses my nape.

"It's beautiful," I murmur as I turn to kiss him. "And perfect." His lips are warm and soft, just like his heart.

"Mama!" Avery's impatient voice cuts through our moment. "More pesents!"

I sigh and shrug.

It's her day, after all.

She tears through present after present, paper lining the floor of the living room. As she's flinging ribbon through the air, Ryan sneaks off and returns with two glasses of mimosas. After handing me one, he joins me on the couch and wraps an arm around my shoulders. Pulling me close, he gently rubs my arm as Avery continues her assault. I sink into the warmth of his side, appreciative of the simple gesture. We sip our cocktails until she's exhausted herself, falling asleep on the floor while clutching one of her many new stuffed animals. We both stand – Ryan moving toward the bathroom, and I toward the kitchen to refill my champagne glass. As I'm mid-pour, a knock at the door startles me and I nearly drop my glass.

I'm not expecting anyone – we're going to Faith's for dinner later on this afternoon.

Moving to the door, I peer outside.

There's no one there.

Looking closer, I notice a box on the porch wrapped in pretty holiday paper.

Someone must have sent Avery a Christmas gift. I can't imagine who. We'll see both my and Ryan's parents at the wedding this weekend. I twist my lips as I open the door. Bending down, I pick it up and bring it into the kitchen. The tag tied to the outside has my name on it.

I smile. Ryan is obviously up to no good. I wonder if I should wait for him to open it... my curiosity gets the better of me, and I tear into the paper. The box is taped well, so I fish a butter knife from the drawer and skate it along the seams. Moving the flaps, I peer inside and scream, dropping the butter knife. It falls to the floor in a loud clank. I stand in front of the present with my hands over my face, trying to control the high-pitched screeches emanating from my throat.

"Abigail!" Ryan flies into the kitchen and stops dead in his tracks when he sees me standing over the box.

Still not able to form words, I point to it, my arm tremoring from my shoulder to the tip of my nail. Carefully, he approaches it and looks inside. He reaches in and retrieves a backpack – Avery's baby blue polka-dotted preschool backpack. Not a similar looking one, but her *exact* backpack.

It's like an invisible hand is clasped over my mouth with a ghostly hypodermic of adrenaline piercing my heart.

Ryan tosses it on the counter and races up the stairs, but I'm still unable to move.

He's going to check for what I already know isn't there.

I know this is hers.

There's a heart keychain I placed on one of the straps just the other day, and it's dangling on this backpack right where I left it.

She saw it in the store and pointed to it, so I bought it. I put it there so she knows we love her, even though she's not with us. I can't tear my eyes away from that tiny, dangling heart.

He bounds back down and into the kitchen. "I hung it up last night, before you read her the story," I whisper in horror, still staring at it. I lift my head to Ryan, tears threatening to spray from my eyes. "How?"

Ryan's jaw clenches. He shakes his head in disbelief, then begins to unzip the bag. Inside are all of her belongings, plus one additional paper folded into quarters. "Fuck," he breathes as he places it on the counter, then begins to search around the kitchen. He opens drawer after drawer until he finds what he was searching for – a pair of gloves. Putting them on, he returns to the folded paper and begins to unfold it. Inside is a picture of me with a hand-drawn noose around my neck. Panic begins to set in like a cluster of spark plugs in my abdomen.

Who?

Who would do this?

The thoughts are accelerating inside my head like a runaway freight train. I want them to slow so I can breathe, but they won't. My breaths come in gasps – my ribs heaving as if bound by ropes, straining to inflate my lungs. The room begins to spin around and around. I squat on the floor, trying to make everything slow to something my brain and body can cope with.

Ryan's at my side within seconds of me hitting

the floor. He sits and pulls my body into his so he's cradling me. "Shhhh," he coos. "I won't let anything happen to you or Avery." I lay my head against his chest and concentrate on his heartbeat.

Lub-dub.

Lub-dub.

My head is a carousel of fears spinning out of control, each one pushing my mind into blackness.

Lub-dub.

My heart hammers inside my chest like it belongs to a rabbit running for its life.

Lub-dub.

Ryan begins to hum a song, I'm not sure what it is, but it's beginning to calm me. He sways me back and forth until my body stops tremoring. Shifting so we're facing each other, he cradles my face in his hands. "I won't let anyone hurt you," he repeats, wiping a stray tear from my cheek with his thumb. "Do you believe that?"

His eyes search mine for an answer. My heart believes every word that Ryan has ever breathed. My head. That's where the problem lies. I know he'd stand in front of a bullet for me. But he can't be with me and Avery every second of every day.

"I do." My voice sounds foreign to my own ears as if I'm standing on the outside looking in.

He stands, bringing me with him. "I'm going to go put this back upstairs where it belongs," he begins, taking the backpack off the counter. "Then I'm going to check all of the windows and doors. When Avery wakes, we'll leave for Faith's. I want the two of you to spend the night there while I do some investigating around here." The authoritative Navy SEAL just took over Ryan, and I know there's no arguing with him when he takes that role.

CHAPTER 6

Ryan

"Avery will be up soon. I should get dressed." Her voice comes out thin and distant. There's a haziness in her eyes as she takes a few steps forward, bumping into the kitchen counter like she wasn't expecting it. Her head rolls with the impact, eyes glazed.

Motherfucker.

I'll break every bone in Richard's body just so I can watch him suffer for what he's done to my Montana.

I move to help her, but she shakes me off. She's

still reeling from that fucking package. I'm not sure what scares her more – the fact that someone got in here last night and took her backpack, or the noose around her photo.

I can't figure out how someone got in here undetected. I locked all of the doors myself. I watch as Montana stumbles into the bedroom then closes the door gently behind her.

Motherfucker.

I ripped off the gloves when she slid to the floor, so I need to put on a fresh pair. If I'm lucky, this asshole made a mistake and there's some trace of DNA on the page. Gloving up, I find a Ziploc bag and place the photo inside. Then I rush up the stairs, hanging Avery's backpack where it belongs.

I move from room to room and check each window and lock, but they're all sealed. There's no way he could have gotten in this way. Tilting my head down the stairwell, I check for any noise. Hearing none, I march into my office and close the door. I need to call Nate.

He picks up on the second ring. "Merry Christmas, Ryan," he answers.

"No, not really," I growl. "We're coming early, and we need to talk."

His tone changes in an instant. "What happened?"

"I'll explain when I get there. Have a go-bag packed. We may be making an unscheduled trip."

WITHIN AN HOUR, I have the car packed and both girls ready to go. The drive isn't long, but Faith and Cade don't live around the corner either. Avery, oblivious of the events that occurred during her nap, sings to herself in the backseat, while Abigail is unusually quiet. I know thoughts are spinning wildly inside her head, and it pisses me off. One way or another, I'll have an end to this shit before the wedding.

Another hour and we arrive at their place. Faith ushers the girls in while I grab the presents and small bag I packed for them. Cade jogs outside to help.

"Girls are staying here for a couple of days," I command. "Grab those boxes and meet me outside by the pool."

I sling Avery's duffel bag over my shoulders and stride inside. Once I get them settled, I storm out the back door and toward the back of the pool where the gazebo is. Cade is waiting for me as I instructed.

"What happened?" he asks again, his brow furrowed.

I explain all the events that transpired, watching his reaction in real-time.

His facial expressions morph from confused to angry.

Very angry.

Good.

I need him just as pissed as I am to fix this.

"What now?" he asks, pacing around the small octagonal structure.

I lean against one of the uprights. "Tomorrow, we take the note and the box the backpack was wrapped in down to the base. A buddy of mine knows a couple of FBI forensic investigators. I'm going to try and fast track DNA and fingerprints." I pause, then sigh. "I have a gut feeling though, that we won't find any."

He shrugs. "Could be whoever did it could be sloppy."

"True, but I don't think this was done by some novice B&E guy. This screams pro. Besides the DNA, there must be some kind of money trail.

We're you able to get any information on the asshole ex-father-in-law?"

He shakes his head. "Still waiting. Hoping to hear something tomorrow."

I run my fingers through my hair and frown. "I still can't figure out how he got into the house. All of the doors and windows, and I mean *all* of them, were locked."

He scratches his chin. "Is it possible someone could have made a copy of the house key?"

I shake my head. "I can't see how. I never leave them anywhere, and unless someone took them from Montana's bag…"

"It is possible, though," he insists.

I exit the gazebo. "Let's go find out." We both walk back to the house and find Abigail and Faith in the kitchen. "Babe, where's your purse?"

She motions to a location behind me. "On the table over there." I turn my head to where she's signaling to and approach her purse. As I'm rummaging through the bag, she asks, "Why?"

"Where are your keys?" Her bag isn't that big, yet I don't see her keys.

Standing, she moves toward me. "They should be in there. Why are you asking?" She repeats the question with more force.

I keep looking. "They're not here. When was the last time you remember having them?" I ask, lifting my head from the purse.

She tilts her head to the side. "Faith and I went to get our nails done the other day. She drove, but I remember putting my keys in my bag." She snatches the bag from my grip. Turning to the kitchen island, she dumps out the contents on the counter. Plenty of typical things fly out – wallet, Chapstick, nail file – but no keys. "I don't understand..." She trails off.

"When you were getting your nails done, did you have your purse with you the entire time?"

Sitting back down, she twirls the ends of her hair around her finger. "Now that I think about it, no. It was hanging on the back of my chair, and I had to get up and wash my hands." She frowns. "But I was only gone for a minute or two."

"That's all it takes," Cade mutters.

That would explain how someone had gotten in undetected.

I need to install a security system immediately.

Faith stands up. "I don't understand. Who would want to break into your house?"

Unsure of what Montana told her sister, I answer, "We're not sure, but I'm sure as hell gonna find out." I'm not thrilled someone took her keys, but it makes sense. "Where's Avery?" I don't hear her, and that's usually not a good sign.

Faith answers. "I gave her one of her presents to tide her over until you two got finished with whatever it was you were doing outside. She's in the living room playing with it."

I peek my head around the door frame and find Avery on the floor with a very large dollhouse. I turn back to Faith and narrow my eyes. She smiles and shrugs.

"Just remember," I mutter almost to myself, "Payback is a bitch."

She better hope when she and Cade have kids, they have boys. Uncle Ryan *will* find the biggest stuffed bear and make sure any little girl they have owns at least one.

As much as it will pain me to put this almost full-size house in the back of my truck, she's content and having a good time which makes me happy.

I move toward Montana, who's still staring at the contents of her purse that are scattered all over the counter. "I should have never—"

"Don't," I murmur as I come up behind her. "Don't start second-guessing yourself. They could be on the table at home and you don't remember taking them out of your bag." I press my front against her back and place my arms around her. She leans her head on my chest. "Please, don't worry. That's my job." Leaning in, I place a gentle kiss on her cheek.

"C'mon. Let's let Avery finish opening her gifts, or we'll be up all night," Cade insists with a laugh. Montana smiles, but it doesn't reach her eyes.

Motherfucker.

EARLY THE NEXT MORNING, Cade and I jump in the truck and head to San Diego. One of my contacts at the base called ahead, and Mr. Edward Matthews in the San Diego field office is expecting us.

We need to figure this out, and fast. I have Mateo keeping an eye on the house, unbeknownst to Montana and Faith. If he does his job the way I know he can, they'll never know he's there. I don't want to burden them with the fact that I'm nervous enough to enlist one of my employees to watch them. If anyone as much as sneezes in their direction, I'll know about it.

On the drive, we discuss strategy.

"What if it's not who you think it is?" Cade muses.

I shake my head. "No. It has to be him. Who else would want to hurt Montana this way? She has no enemies." She is the most caring, compassionate person I've ever met, and I can't see anyone else want to hurt her. I press my foot harder on the gas. "We just need to prove it's Richard."

He shifts in his seat. "Alright. We prove it's him. Then what? For all intents and purposes, we're civilians. We need to go through the proper channels."

He's right – which is why I have someone useful in Eagle Rock.

"Don't worry about that. I have those bases covered."

Fifteen minutes later, we pull up to a large building made almost entirely of windows. It was erected just a few years ago, and it still has that sparkling new appearance. We park out front and stroll to the entrance.

The inside of the building is bright – the massive Federal Bureau of Investigation seal prominently placed directly in front of you as you walk in. We both step up to the officer at the front desk.

He looks up from his computer and asks us for our credentials. Cade and I are ready and have them on the counter before he can count to three. Taking them, he looks them over and hands them back, then directs us to the brown leather couches and asks us to wait there.

It isn't five minutes before someone exits the elevator and escorts us upstairs to the fourth floor. We pass a few closed doors before entering an open one on the right.

"Please take a seat," the agent states, motioning to the chairs in front of a large desk.

"Thank you," I answer as I take a seat. Cade follows suit. When he's satisfied, he leaves and shuts the door behind him.

Cade whistles through his teeth. "Nice place."

The office is massive. Framed accomplishments hang prestigiously behind it... from photos with past Presidents to awards and accolades. This guy has seen and done it all.

I'm still taking it all in when a man enters the room. Cade and I stand out of habit. "Mr. Kane, I'm Special Agent in Charge Michael Donovan. I run the San Diego Field office."

He extends a hand and I shake it. "This is my partner, Cade McCall." They shake, and Donovan walks around to his chair.

"I understand you need some assistance?" he asks, placing his arms on the desk.

I nod. I give him a brief rundown what's been happening, and finish with, "Any help you can give us would be greatly appreciated."

"You have friends in very high places." He chuckles as he stands. "My lab is at your disposal. Let me introduce you to one of my top lab technicians, Catherine." He moves toward the door and escorts us down the hall to a lab room. A petite blonde in a white coat sits behind some large piece of equipment.

"Cat, this is Ryan and Cade. Whatever they need, make happen."

She smiles. "Of course, sir."

"You're in very capable hands, gentlemen," Donovan announces as he takes his leave.

As the door closes, Catherine stands. "So, what is it you're looking to have done."

I place a small plastic bag filled with the items I need run on the counter. She peeks in, then lifts her head from the bag. "For purposes of searching through CODIS, Rapid DNA systems are not authorized for use on crime scene samples. It's not compliant with the FBI Director's Quality Assurance Standards. I'm not even supposed to run this through at all," she murmurs, but adds, "But I will. That being said, it won't hold up in court unless I send it off to the lab – which I'll do with the rest of the sample."

I nod, completely understanding her predicament. "Not a problem. This is more for preliminary identification, to make sure we're looking in the right direction."

She gloves up, then takes both the box and the sealed note to her work station. "Do you have a DNA sample to compare this to?"

"No," I answer as I shake my head. "However, there should be a familial match in the system. Daniel Murphy was incarcerated, so his DNA should be in CODIS."

She nods. "Take a seat, this is going to take a few." Both Cade and I sit as she checks the note for fingerprints and DNA. We watch as she meticulously examines the box and the backpack swabbing for DNA, and the note which she checks for fingerprints.

She places something under a microscope off to the side of the lab. "I found what appears to be a hair," she announces as she peers into the lens. "But no follicle attached, so that's no good."

Removing that slide, she turns back to a large machine behind her. "I was able to lift a single print off of the paper. Honestly, my guess is the perp wore gloves when handling and signing the paper when he placed it in the box but didn't when he originally took the paper out of the packaging." She hits a few buttons. "I'm running it through CODIS now."

"That's good, right?" I blurt.

Shaking her head, she answers, "Not necessarily. If he's not printed, they won't come up."

She re-examines the envelope the note was sealed in and takes a swab out of a sterile bag. Extracting distilled water from a vial using a sterile pipette, she applies one drop to the side of the tip. "I'm hoping he licked the envelope to seal it. As careful as some people are, some forget about that part." She then applies the tip to the envelope and rubs using moderate pressure while rotating the swab to ensure the entire surface has made contact with it. "I bet my life there's remnant DNA here." Moving to the opposite side of the room, she cuts the tip of the swab off and places it in a test tube. She opens the microwave sized machine and inserts the tube into a holder.

"How long before you know?" I ask, mesmerized with the science. I glance at Cade, who's fixated on the machine as well.

She shrugs. "Depends. Could take minutes, could take hours." She hits a few buttons on the touch screen and it begins to make noise. "Once the analysis is done, it will be uploaded to CODIS." The machine beeps and the screen lights up. "Well now," she murmurs as she looks at the information that scrolls across the small screen. "Turns out both a Daniel Murphy and a Richard Murphy are in CODIS."

I chuckle. "No shit?" I mutter under my breath.

"Hmmm," she continues, still looking at the screen.

"What does it say?" Cody asks, moving closer.

She frowns. "So, there was definitely DNA on the envelope," she begins as she writes a few things down.

"But?" I ask, clenching my teeth.

"It's not a paternal match to your inmate." She looks again, then says, "It's more like a sibling. There are matches, but not enough to make it father-son." She moves out of the way and points to the screen. "Okay, so father and son will have fifty percent or so of the same DNA. This sample compared to the one in CODIS has about that, but the markers aren't the same to the father. Siblings also share about fifty percent, but they will have slightly different markers from each other."

I furrow my brow. "Holy shit. That asshole has a brother or sister?"

She turns and faces us. "Brother. Definitely male DNA."

Cade spins toward me. "Does Danny have a brother?"

"Not as far as I know," I answer, running my fingers through my hair. "I've never seen or heard of a brother."

That sets off a red flag.

Alarm bells ring loudly through my head.

If Danny does have a brother, why has Montana never mentioned it?

I move toward the door. "This is fantastic. Thank you so much for all of your hard work." I signal to Cade. "We gotta go. We got work to do."

Cade waves to Catherine. "Thanks again," he says as we take our leave.

Down the elevator and back through the glass-walled entryway, we exit the building.

Once outside, I snap. "What the actual fuck. A goddamn brother who may as well be a ghost." That explains the lack of a money trail.

"Shit," Cade mutters, trying to keep up with my jog to the truck.

We get in and I roar out of the parking lot. "I need to make a phone call." Using my steering wheel, I navigate to my address book and dial Tanner's number. He answers on the second ring. "Hey, Ryan. Everything alright?"

"No," I growl. "I need to know – does Danny have a brother?"

A heavy sigh comes through the speakers. "You can say that."

"Explain," I demand as I get on the freeway.

"Alright, but you asked for it," he mutters. "Danny has a fraternal twin brother, Dillon. He was never really quite right in the head. They say the umbilical cord was wrapped around his neck and there was oxygen deprivation just before birth." He pauses for a moment, then continues. "He was in and out of schools, not one able to deal with his behavioral issues. His father finally admitted him to a psych ward when he tried to stab one of his teachers through the eye with a pencil. Lucky for her, he missed."

"Holy shit," Cade utters, his eyebrows shooting up.

"He was six."

I clench my jaw. "Fucking six," I mutter almost to myself.

Tanner releases an awkward chuckle. "You can see why this never came up as dinner conversation."

I jump in. "Does Montana—"

"No one knows. The only reason I know is because the teacher he tried to stab was my aunt. This was kept a secret from everyone, and those who knew Danny was a twin was told Dillon died." He pauses again, then asks, "Why are you asking me this?"

"Christmas morning, a present was left on the doorstep. Assuming it was for Avery, Abigail opened it and found Avery's backpack. The exact same backpack that was hanging in her room the night before."

"Ohmigod," he whispers in horror.

"Exactly," I mutter. "We just left the FBI field office in San Diego and found the DNA from the envelope that accompanied the present, had familial DNA matches to both Danny and Richard." I opt not to tell him about what the letter said. He's been friends with Montana for a while, and I don't want him to worry too.

"That's impossible," he argues. "Dillon is under the care of the state of Montana. He's never to be released."

I scratch the back of my neck. "I'm just telling you what the DNA is telling us, and DNA doesn't lie."

"Let me make a few phone calls, and I'll get back to you," he insists.

"Alright," I answer and hang up.

Cade shifts in his seat so he's facing me. "Do you think he was released or managed to escape?"

"Not sure," I answer. "But I'm sure Tanner's wondering that exact question right now." Pulling into the driveway, I place the truck in park. I reach over and grab Cade's arm, who's about to exit. He turns his head so we're looking at one another. "Don't mention any of this to the girls. I need to work a few things out first."

He nods in understanding. The last thing I want to do is freak Montana out and finding out she has an ex-brother-in-law who's certifiably insane might just push her over the edge.

We walk into the house – Cade goes to find Faith, and I head upstairs. I'll talk to Montana after

I've done some research. Firing up the laptop, I do a search for Dillon Murphy. Page after page of complaints fill my screen but end around the mid-nineteen nineties. I keep digging until I find what I'm looking for... an unidentified man escaped from the Plainedge Psychiatric Facility, which is located just a few miles outside of Eagle Rock, two weeks ago. As I open up the article, my phone rings. It's Tanner.

I answer with a question. "He escaped, didn't he?"

"I just confirmed it with the facility," he affirms.

Now the question is, did Richard know. "I found an article stating as much, but the man is unidentified."

"Richard likes to keep his family drama private," Tanner mutters. "Or as much as he can control."

I lean the arch of my back into the chair, stretching out my sore muscles. I haven't been to the gym ever since we were almost run off the road, and I'm paying for it now. The stress from recent circumstances isn't helping my lower back any. "But you know for a fact that it's him."

"Yeah. I have a friend who works in the facility."

I tap my fingers on the desk, my thoughts

running wild. "Is this a common occurrence? How is it a man who's clearly dangerous to others isn't supervised at all times?"

He sighs into the phone. "The guard who was tasked to watch him stepped away for a few minutes."

"Stepped away? How convenient." That doesn't make any sense, unless... "Can we check into the guard's financials? I have a sneaking suspicion he stepped away and was paid to do so."

"My thoughts exactly," he concurs. Papers rustle in the background. "That's what I was doing right before I called you, and I just got his bank statements." He pauses for a few minutes, then adds, "There is a deposit of ten thousand dollars from an LLC that was made two days before Dillon escaped."

Motherfucker. "What's the name of the company?"

"Rexport."

CHAPTER 7

Abigail

RYAN'S BEEN UPSTAIRS in Cade's office for hours, and it worries me.

The fact that I can't stay in my own home, worries me.

The fact that my daughter's backpack wound up on the porch in a box... worries me.

But we leave for Mammoth Mountain in a couple of days and I have to pack.

And do laundry.

And put the dozens of gifts Avery received in her room.

And a hundred other stupid errands that need to be done before we leave, like picking up my wedding dress and Ryan's tux. He won't let me go anywhere alone, so I'll have to drag him around to do all of my chores.

That should be fun.

Just as I was about to stomp upstairs and demand he come down, he makes an appearance at the bottom of the steps.

"What have you been doing?" I ask in more of a demanding tone than I mean.

"Last minute details, my love," he answers, then kisses me on my forehead.

His haunted expression along with the smile that doesn't reach his eyes tell me otherwise. "Anything I can help you with?"

He shakes his head. "I have it all under control." Moving closer, he places his arms around me. "Just a few more days, and you'll be Mrs. Ryan Kane."

I smile just thinking about it. I know it's stupid – I mean, it's just a name – but knowing that in a short few days he'll be mine legally makes me happy.

"The hours can't go by fast enough," I assure him.

He leans his forehead against mine and sighs.

There's definitely something he's not telling me, and it pains me to see him upset. I place my cheek on his chest and hold him tight, hoping whatever it is he's keeping from me isn't dangerous.

DRAGGING RYAN from errand to errand the past couple of days wasn't as bad as I thought it would be.

No moaning or complaining.

No hurry up.

If I didn't know any better, I'd think he was enjoying himself.

I was able to get everything done with time to spare, which is rare when you're dragging around a toddler. He was the perfect time saver.

Ryan finally allowed us to go back to the house last night. I'd packed up everything we needed, and early that next morning we're on the move.

The scenic trip lasted just over nine hours with several potty and food stops, but when I see the resort... I realize it was worth the drive. As a child, I dreamed of a winter wonderland wedding, complete with roaring fireplaces and pillows of snow. This exceeds my expectations.

We pull up to a wooden fantasyland encased in a backdrop of snow-capped mountains. The Sierra Lodge is picturesque with a maroon and brown exterior, peaked roofs and wooden balconies stretching across the face of the building, giving that log cabin feel. Ryan maneuvers the truck to the entrance and I step out to retrieve Avery. As he's unloading all of our luggage, I take Avery inside where it's a bit warmer. When I enter, my eyes widen and my mouth hangs open.

It's as if I stepped into a movie set, it's that perfect.

It exudes a casual elegance with high ceilings, a wall of windows, and rich wood paneling. Grand chandeliers dangle over our heads, lighting the slate tile floor that extends throughout the room. I wander around the colossal space toward the reception desk that's directly to my left, with the word "Sierra" written in massive cursive serving as a backdrop.

Still holding Avery who's exhausted from the trip, I move toward what appears to be a lower lobby. So, I descend a grand staircase and toward windows that take up an entire wall. There's an area that matches outside; a quiet lodge-like space with stone fireplaces, antique-looking armchairs, and stone floors. We'll need to have a cocktail and really get to know our surroundings later.

I shuffle back upstairs to find Ryan checking us in. Our luggage is being pushed toward a bank of elevators by a resort employee. After he's handed over his credit card, he saunters over to us.

"This place looks better than the pictures," he brags.

This is all his idea, and he did the research on the resort. I smile and nod. "Yes, it does. You did good," I tease.

Ryan moves toward the elevators, and I follow him. Avery begins to squirm, so I put her down and allow her to walk next to Ryan. Once we stop, she tugs on his pant leg.

"Wyan, I tiwed," she whines, then lifts her hands up.

He scoops her up without a second thought. She places her tiny arms around his neck and leans her head on his chest. I wouldn't be surprised if she's fast asleep before the elevator doors open. As soon as the bell sounds, her eyes are closed.

"I still don't know how you do it," I whisper as we enter.

"It's a gift," he jests with a grin.

I move to the back of the car. "My parents are

flying in tomorrow morning. She can spend some time with them – I want to walk around the village."

"Whatever my bride desires."

EARLY THE NEXT MORNING, the three of us head downstairs for breakfast. My parents will be here around ten, so that gives us plenty of time to eat and relax before my anxiety kicks up. My mom means well, but living in Colorado means she doesn't get to see me or Avery much. She'll want to take control of everything. I'm glad Ryan did most of the work – he can deal with my mother's controlling demeanor.

Just outside the resort is a miniature village with shops and restaurants. With the large mountain as a background, it's reminiscent of Switzerland. There's a main street made of cobblestones where skiers and tourist alike walk from shop to shop. Fire pits are along either side of the walk, and people huddle around them for warmth.

This is the one thing I miss.

I love living in California and I wouldn't move back to Montana, but there's just something about the crisp air and beautiful snowy mountain views that I'll always crave.

We finish breakfast and head back to the hotel. Ryan takes Avery to the arcade that's off the lobby to play a few games of pinball. I sit on the couch next to the fireplace and wait. Checking my watch, I notice the time is just about ten, so they should be here any minute.

Out of nowhere I shiver, the wave going all the way to my feet – the roaring fire next to me not able to stop it. The hair on the back of my neck stand straight up and that feeling of being watched is back. I scan the hotel searching for anything out of the ordinary, but don't see anyone looking in my direction. The lobby is busy, but everyone is immersed in their own activities.

"Abigail!" a female voice sings from my right.

A voice that gives me palpitations.

My mother.

Turning my head, I find my parents standing in the middle of the lobby like statues. People have to walk around them to get in or out of the hotel. I stand and wave them toward me. My father gets to me first, giving me a hug and kissing the top of my head. He's been doing this since I was a kid and hasn't stopped even though I'm almost as tall as he is.

My mother is more subtle about her affections. "The flight was murder," she begins as she drops her bag on the floor at my father's feet. "But, we're here."

"We wouldn't miss this for the world, honey." He glances at my mother and shoots her a stop-the-shit glare.

She shrugs and continues. "The resort is very pretty. I hope the rooms are just as nice as the lobby."

Oh for Christ's sake.

"Where's my favorite granddaughter?" my dad asks, looking around the massive space.

I roll my eyes. "She's your only granddaughter."

"She's still my favorite," he insists with a wink.

"Ryan has her in the arcade. I'll text him that you're here." I pull my phone from my back jeans pocket and text him.

Within a few minutes, they're walking through the lobby. Avery sees my parents and wriggles out of Ryan's arms and runs straight for my father. They haven't seen her physically in almost two years, but we FaceTime at least once a week.

"There she is!" my father sings and squats down

to Avery's height. She runs right into his arms. Scooping her up, he places a giant kiss on her cheek. "How's my girl?"

"Hi gwampa!" she squeals as she throws her arms around his neck.

"We missed you, Avery," my mom insists, and moves to kiss her on the cheek.

She giggles. "Miss you too."

Ryan moves to stand next to me. "Mr. and Mrs. Montana, it's a pleasure to finally meet you."

Shifting Avery to his left arm, my dad extends his right hand. "We've heard nothing but great things about you."

"And our Abby looks happy, now," her mother adds. "But please, call me Barbara."

My dad nods in agreement. "Mr. Montana is so formal. Ben works just fine."

"Alright, Barbara and Ben," Ryan chuckles. "Why don't we get you settled upstairs."

A hotel employee comes by and asks if they need help with their bags. "That would be great. I'm going to check in now," my dad answers.

Ryan shakes his head. "No need, it's already taken care of. They're in room four-oh-six."

"Everything is paid for," I tell my parents. "We're across the hall in four-oh-five."

My father frowns. "That wasn't necess—"

"I know, but we wanted to do it," I cut him off before he goes on a tirade.

My mother smiles, knowing arguing with me isn't going to get them anywhere. She knows where I got my stubborn streak from. "Thank you."

"Don't worry," I tease, "we'll just call it payment for services rendered in babysitting fees."

I decide not to mention the creepy feeling to Ryan – at least, not now. The last thing I need is for him to go bat shit crazy and cover this place in former SEALs. I want a semi-relaxed wedding and reception. We'll deal with the crazy another day.

CHAPTER 8

Ryan

HER PARENTS SEEM NICE.

I'm glad they could make it.

The least I could do is pay for the room since they refused to let me pay for their flights.

I think they would have gotten along with my parents, if they were still here.

The only comforting thought is they went out together, and they didn't feel any pain – or at least that's what I was told.

I was on a deployment at the time of their crash. I came home for the funeral, but had to go right back. I don't regret not spending a little more time home before going back to Afghanistan. I had no siblings to console, no other close family to commiserate with.

My team needed me.

They're my family.

My brothers.

They were still living and there was nothing I could do sitting at home.

If I hadn't gone back when I did...

Tonight is the rehearsal dinner with the ceremony tomorrow. Barbara and Ben want to take Avery for lunch so Montana and I can do a little shopping. Everyone else is coming in by dinner, so this will be the only real alone time we have before all of the festivities start. Cade and Faith are meeting us for lunch across the square in an hour, so Montana wants to do a little souvenir shopping first.

We walk through store after store as she picks up little trinkets for friends and family who are coming tonight. As we enter the last store before heading over to lunch, something catches my attention. Out of the corner of my eye, I notice a man standing off to the side. He's been lurking since we entered the first store, but I thought he was shopping the same as us.

I glance over at him to find he's watching us.

Watching Montana.

Without drawing suspicion, I maneuver around the small store to get a better look at the guy. Then it hits me – the nose, the shape of his eyes... it's Dillon.

He's here.

That motherfucker is here.

Fuck. I can't go chasing after the guy without drawing attention. And I'm sure as hell not letting Montana out of my sight. So, I call Cade while casually looking at touristy items. "I'm at the gift shop across from the restaurant. I need you to covertly get into the store. Dillon's here."

"You're fucking kidding?" he whispers.

I frown. "I wish I was. We need to end this. Now."

"I'll be there in thirty seconds."

"Wait outside. I'm going to try and draw him out. He's wearing a blue baseball cap with a black coat and jeans."

"Copy that," he answers, and the line goes dead.

Putting my cell phone in my back pocket, I side

step closer to Montana. "Hey babe, it's time for lunch."

She checks her watch. "Oh, I lost track of time." She puts the mug she was looking at back on the shelf. "We'll come back after. There's some really nice things here."

I smile. "Anything my baby wants."

Taking her hand, I lead her out of the store. Just as I thought, Dillon follows a distance behind. I need to make sure she's clear of him before circling back to help Cade. We walk into the restaurant and I spot Faith sitting at a booth on the far end.

"Hey, I need to use the men's room. Why don't you go and sit with Faith. I'll be right back." I place a kiss on her forehead, then she turns toward Faith. Once I see her sit, I head back to the front of the restaurant and exit.

I scan the crowd, searching for either Dillon or Cade.

I don't see either one.

Where the fuck could they have gone?

Then I see it.

A blue baseball cap running through the crowds of people, with Cade trying to catch it. I sprint after both of them, managing to catch up with Cade. "Where did he go?" I pant as I reach him.

He points to his right. "Around that corner."

We both take off, rounding the corner. The street is empty, with no sign of Dillon. We move slow – from what we know of him, he's dangerous. There's an alley to the right, so Cade and I move to the wall just before the entrance. "I don't know if he's armed," I whisper.

"I'll go first, you cover my six." He peers around the corner. "Ready?"

I nod. He turns the corner and I follow a few steps behind, keeping an eye on our backs. This alley is a dead end, but there are several doors he could have ran into. Just as Cade's about to open one, a noise from the back of the alley catches our attention. A random box falls from the top of a dumpster.

There's no breeze, and no one around to have pushed it off.

I glance over at Cade. "I saw it too," he murmurs. "You go left – I'll go right."

I nod, and we move in separate directions.

Before we reach the back of the dumpster, Dillon jumps up and tries to run past us. Cade spins and launches himself through the air, and lands on a scrambling Dillon.

Dillon manages to squirm his way out of Cade's hold and backs up against the wall. Reaching into his back waistband, he retrieves a combat knife. "Don't do anything stupid, Dillon," I warn him. "It's two against one, and we're trained military combatants."

His eyes are wild – his grip on the knife shaking. He's one loose bolt away from completely falling apart. "You. Killed. My. Brother," he growls.

In this frozen second between stand off and fighting, I see his eyes flick from me to Cade.

Our faces are unreadable – no fear, no invitational smirk.

I'm banking on him to make a costly mistake, and I'm not disappointed.

He launches himself at me, swinging the knife erratically toward my throat. I back up a step as he lunges, the knife missing me by inches. He tries to spin around, but the miss puts him off balance. Moving to my right, I reach out with my left hand and grab his wrist, squeezing until the blade falls from his useless grip.

I glance over at Cade, who's standing in the ready position.

Shaking my head subtly, he stands down.

I return my attention to Dillon. "This is for Montana," I snarl. Thrusting my elbow toward Dillon, my forearm strikes him in the head and knocks him sideways. A split second later, I pile drive my knee into his hip, sending him flying into the wall. He reaches out and grabs the collar of my t-shirt before he hits, but I manage to avoid his grasp.

Before Dillon can recover, I'm all over him. My right arm scythes through the air and catches him square in the face, crumpling his nose and cracking his cheek. His head twists as his body moves left from the force.

Rage builds like deep water currents.

Rage burning so bad, it's like fire lacing my veins and creeping up my spine.

I have the overwhelming desire to strangle the life out of this man, but I opt to teach him a lesson instead.

That's what military training does – teaches you to control the urges and take your rage and focus it elsewhere.

I swing my left elbow and connect with his jaw, splitting his lip wide open and dislodging some teeth. Taking fistfuls of shirt, I drag him down so he's hovering over the sidewalk.

"Stop!" a voice from behind us commands. With my hands still gripping Dillon, I turn to look over my shoulder. There, standing at the end of the alley is Richard.

"Why?" I ask, still suspending Dillon over the ground. "He tried to kill both Montana and I. But, you already knew that." I let go of Dillon and he lands with a thud. He coughs, blood spraying from his mangled mouth. He's hurt bad and not going anywhere, so I decide to focus my attention elsewhere.

Standing, I turn toward Richard. "I know, and I'm sorry." His mouth twists – his expression somewhere between self-pity and bitter contempt.

"I don't think you are," I snap back, taking a few steps toward him. Richard stands his ground. Cade moves so he's in between me and Dillon, in case he decides to try something stupid.

"I know it wasn't you who killed my son," he admits.

I clench my jaw. "Yet, you send your psychopathic son to torment an innocent woman and child. What if Avery had opened that box?" My anger increases with every syllable spoken.

"What box?" he questions, then looks down at Dillon. "I don't know anything about a box."

"Stop the shit," I snarl. "The box with Avery's backpack in it?"

His eyes go wide. Moving his gaze from me, he stares down at Dillon, then back to me. "I promise you, I don't have any idea what you're talking about." He takes a step forward, but holds up his hands as a sign of surrender. "I told Dillon to back off. I didn't want little Avery to get hurt."

"He's fucking lucky she wasn't in the car when he tried to run us off the road," I roar, my Irish temper starting to get the better of me.

He nods. "I made sure she wasn't," he blurts. "But I don't know anything about a box or a back-pack. Dillon?"

I shift sideways so they're both in my line of sight. He tries to sit up, and slowly makes his way to a vertical position. "You said you wanted her dead for what she did to Danny," he says, confused. "You said she killed Danny."

"She didn't kill Danny," I answer for Richard. "Danny was in prison for driving drunk with Avery in the car and getting into an accident. She could have died." I turn my attention back to Richard. "It's not her fault he committed suicide."

Richard continues to stare at Dillon. "What about a box, Dillon?"

He stands and leans against the wall, placing his arm around his side and wincing. I probably broke a rib or two. His stare goes from me to Richard. "Abby was getting her nails done, so I took her keys. Had copies made and put them back. I was only—"

"What have I done?" Richard cries, his hands flying to the top of his head. "What have I done?"

"You said you wanted her dead!" Dillon repeats. "You said we'd get Avery!"

Commotion from the entrance to the alley catches my attention. Montana and Faith, along with some police officers stand just behind Richard. He drops to his knees, still mumbling about what he's done.

"Cade, can you explain to the officers what transpired?" I ask as I walk toward Montana.

She looks confused, and I don't blame her. "Ryan?" Moving toward her, I pull her into an embrace. "Are you okay?"

I kiss the top of her head. "Yes, and I'll explain everything later." Releasing her, I hold her at arm's length. "Why don't you and Faith go and have lunch. Cade and I need to talk to the officers. We won't be long. I promise."

She frowns, but I insist. Her lips twist in dismay, but she moves toward Faith and they walk out of the alley and back around the corner.

CHAPTER 9

Abigail

I WAKE up early the next morning, all of the drama from the day before finally behind us. Once Faith and I went back to the restaurant, Ryan and Cade explained everything. I'm still in shock that Danny had a twin brother, but it doesn't surprise me why Richard hid him away. The police arrested Richard and are placing Dillon back in a psychiatric facility, but not in Eagle Rock. They decide to go farther into Montana – somewhere Richard doesn't have any influence over any of the employees.

I'm a bit tired from the rehearsal dinner. It was nice to spend time with friends and family in a relaxed setting. I made sure not to drink so I'd be focused today. I knew I'd need to be up early.

Ryan is already gone – my mother and sister insisting if he were to sleep with me the night before the wedding, he needs to be gone before I wake.

Stupid traditions.

Avery slept with my parents last night to give me time to relax with a cup of coffee before starting to get ready for the festivities.

Throwing on a robe, I make a mug of coffee and step out onto the balcony. Our room faces the mountain, and the view is spectacular from our floor.

I take a seat at the bistro table and sigh as I sip the juice of life.

Just as I place my cup down on the table, there's a brisk tapping on my door.

Christ, I just sat down.

Grimacing as I rise, I shuffle through the room toward the door. Faith stands on the other side, way too chipper for this time of the morning. "You're gonna have to take that coffee to go. It's time to primp you up," she sings as she tugs on my arm.

Her room is a few doors down from mine, so I trudge down the hallway after her.

Once we reach her room, she pushes me into an awaiting chair. Directly across from me is every possible hair and makeup product you could possibly think of, and some you probably haven't.

"Is this really necessary?" I ask, staring at all of the paraphernalia.

"Nothing but the best for my sister," she answers as she picks up a hair clip.

Leaning back in the chair, I close my eyes as her hands begin combing through my blonde tresses. She tugs and twists, my head moving from one side to another. Once she's finished with my hair, she moves on to my makeup. My mother arrives as she's starting to apply the foundation and sits across to watch the show.

Almost two hours later, she puts down the last of the makeup brushes. "There," she sings. "All finished."

With my makeup finished and hair perfect, it's time to put on my dress. My mother helps me into the gown and zips up the back. "Wow," she breathes and spins me around to face her. "You look absolutely beautiful."

I glance into the mirror, almost not recognizing myself. My blonde hair is pinned up in wisps, showing off the back of my dress. She's transformed me into a model. Hopefully I won't cry and ruin her work. "Thank you," I whisper to my mother, who's trying hard not to cry.

"I'm glad you're doing this," she says, dabbing her eye with a tissue. "You deserve the perfect wedding, and it seems as if Ryan is the right man to be doing it with." The fact that she's accepted him and is happy for me speaks volumes. She hated Danny from the moment I met him but said it was my life to live. I see now she was right all along.

Avery bounds in from the other room, her hair in banana curls. She looks like a doll – between the dress and hair, people might mistake her for one. "Look, Mama!" she squeals, showing me a small white basket.

I furrow my brow. "For the petals," my mother divulges, reading my unspoken question.

"Right. Petals." The bridal consultant mentioned something about that, but I had almost forgotten.

My mother takes Avery's hand and moves toward the door. "We'll see you at the altar," she murmurs, then exits.

I follow behind her and almost run into Faith. "Oh, Abby!" she squeals, her expression delighted. "You look so beautiful! Oh, no. I think I'm gonna cry." Her eyes begin to well up.

"Don't," I beg. "You'll make me cry."

A lone tear goes rogue down her cheek. "That dress... it's absolutely perfect!"

I wanted something festive and this dress screams winter wonderland. The light blue satin and tulle gown has embroidered lace that resembles snowflakes.

A loud, gruff throat clearing comes from behind us. My father stands, leaning against the wall. "It's time," he announces. Although he's tough on the exterior, he's a teddy bear underneath. I wouldn't be surprised if by the end of the aisle, he didn't have a tear or two running down his cheeks.

"Thanks, Dad," I murmur through a smile.

He thrusts his hand inside his vest pocket and retrieves a small box. "Your mother and I thought you could use something old. I know it's your second marriage, but..." Smiling, he hands it to me.

I open it and find a pair of earrings. "They were your grandmother's. We thought you should have them."

Nestled within a glimmering halo of round diamonds are round blue sapphires in a prong setting, set in white gold. I vaguely remember my grandmother wearing these to a wedding when I was little.

"They're perfect," I whisper as I remove my diamond studs. Taking the sapphires out of the box, I open the hinge back and put them on.

My father's eyes begin to get glassy. "You're perfect," he responds, taking the studs and the box from me.

"Something old," Faith muses, taking a few steps back to admire me. "And your dress is both blue and new... but you still need something borrowed."

She reaches inside her purse and pulls out a ribbon. Upon further inspection, it isn't just any ribbon. My eyes go wide when I realize what it is. "Where did you get—"

"Who do you think?" she answers with a wink. "I mentioned we needed something borrowed, and he suggested this." She places the ribbon in my hand. I run my fingers over the blue and white fabric that holds Ryan's Navy Cross. "We can put it in your bouquet," she advises. "Oh, the bouquet! Dad, can you go and grab our bouquets?"

He nods. "Where are they?"

Faith points to the room I just exited, and my dad goes to retrieve them. Within a few minutes, he's back with the winter wonderland bouquets Ryan ordered. He hands Faith my oversized bouquet of white blooms and earthy greenery.

She pins the metal to the silk wrapping the stems and smiles. "Now my dear sister, you are officially perfect."

The scent of freesia and evergreen envelop me in a soft mist. Closing my eyes, I inhale deep, enjoying the magical smell.

"Good," my father blurts, interrupting my last-minute meditation. "Let's get this show on the road."

As we walk closer toward the aisle leading me to Ryan, notes of Pachelbel's Canon begin to float through the air. The closer we get, the louder the piano becomes. By the time we're at the edge, the song is over and morphs into Ave Maria.

"That's my cue," Faith announces. "Count to

ten, then follow me." She blows me a kiss and begins to walk down the aisle. Classical music has a calming effect, although I was never a fan of the wedding march. I opted for something a little softer and subtler.

I recognize my cue as the song changes to Prelude in C. A hush falls over the crowd and all I hear are the soothing sounds of Bach.

"You ready?" my dad whispers.

I smile. "I've never been readier."

My dad pulls my hand through his arm and grasps it tight, and we begin our slow march. Gasps from the audience fill my ears as we come into view. Satin draped chairs line the aisle – the crowd of faces focusing on me. My cheeks heat as I take in the congregation assembled for us.

They're here for us.

My eyes drift forward, and I see him at the end of my snowy path.

Ryan stands underneath a trellis overflowing with white flowers.

He turns toward me, his eyes meeting my awed gaze. A mesmerizing deep ocean blue with flecks of silvery light dancing throughout—eyes that have me at his mercy.

His face breaks into a smile of exultation. His breathtaking smile – this is what keeps me going.

We reach the end of the aisle, and Ryan holds out his hand. My father, being old-school, takes my hand and places it in Ryan's. We turn toward the justice of the peace as my father takes his seat.

We used simple, traditional vows. Vows that I swear I'll never break in a million years. Ryan and I turn to each other and repeat after the justice of the peace, sealing our commitment with "I do."

The second we're declared husband and wife, Ryan cradles my face in his hands, tears beginning to well in his eyes. He bends his head toward mine, and I stretch on the tips of my toes to reach him. I throw my arms around his neck as our lips meet, and the world melts around us.

The only thing that matters in this moment is us.

ROARING FIREPLACES, spiced beverages, and pillows of untouched snow create a romantic atmosphere for our reception. It's a scene worthy of royalty.

The spacious room is filled with circular

skirted tables partnered with rustic ballroom chairs. Almost everything was white – from the silk tablecloths to the hydrangea floral arrangements surrounded by candles centered on the table. The only splashes of color are the beautiful gowns the women wore. In the center of the room was an area to dance with our table on the outer edge along the wall of windows and the massive fireplace on the other.

Ryan and I stand just outside the dining area, waiting to be announced. I peek around the corner, anxious to get this party started. The room buzzes with excited chatter as children run between the tables playing a game of tag, Avery being the ringleader. I'm glad to see she's having fun. "Ladies and gentlemen, let's give a round of applause to the new Mr. and Mrs. Ryan Kane!" the DJ announces from behind his stage.

"That's our cue, Mrs. Kane," Ryan whispers with a wink. As we enter, applause spreads across the room. Chairs scrape across the wood floor as guests get up for a standing ovation. With a huge smile on my face, we stride to the center of the dance floor. It's time for the traditional first dance.

The DJ strikes up the song we chose: Christina

Perri's "A Thousand Years." Ryan makes me feel nothing short of a queen as he places his arms around me and holds me close. I melt into his arms as he sways back and forth in time with the music. Halfway through the song, the DJ invites the small wedding party up to dance, then the rest of the guests. We're soon surrounded by everyone we love. Avery comes running over, and Ryan scoops her up. Extending her arm, he takes her tiny hand and dances with her in circles, moving her with the song. My heart swells more than I thought possible at the beautiful sight.

The song ends and everyone applauds once again. Ryan places Avery down and extends his hand out to me. I take it and we move slowly toward our table. Just as we're about to sit, Ryan takes the back of my hand and places a gentle kiss on my skin. He's grinning from ear to ear like a child about to get what he wants. I can't help but smile back.

We sit in front of a bouquet of white anemones with cedar boughs sprawled across the front of the table. Ryan leans in for a kiss, which is followed with cheers. After a few moments, everyone sits down, with the exception of Michael. The sound of his teaspoon rapping on the side of his wineglass signals everyone to be quiet, except the children who are shushed by their parents.

He moves closer to Ryan and I. "I've known Irish here almost fifteen years, twelve of those as active Navy SEALs. We've seen our share of action, had our share of heartbreaks." He pauses, looking at Ryan for a minute, then continues. "He's more than just someone I worked with, he's my brother. The fact that my brother found someone to spend the rest of his life with... I couldn't be happier with his choice. She's an amazing woman, Irish." He raises his glass, and the rest of the guests follow suit. "Here's to my brother and his amazing new wife. May they have many years of happiness. Cheers!"

"Cheers!" everyone chants, then sips their champagne.

I look at Ryan, love swimming in his eyes. "You're the best thing that ever happened to me, Ryan Irish Kane."

He smiles and shakes his head. "No, baby. You got that backward." He places a gentle, loving kiss on my lips. "Having you in my life makes me feel like everything's possible in this world, like I can conquer anything." He cups my cheeks with his palms. "I thank God every day he put you in my life, and I don't know what I'd do without you."

"Well," I answer in between tender kisses. "I guess it's a good thing you'll never have to find out."

The End

ABOUT KATE KINSLEY

Kate Kinsley is the pen name of an Amazon best-selling author who's gone incognito. She loves to write contemporary and military romance, but her passion is romantic suspense. Books with heart-pounding action, adrenaline-inducing chases, edge-of-your-seat thrills, life-threatening situations, and dangerous criminals are what she does best.

Besides being a mom and wife, Kinsley loves spending time with her blue-eyed puppy, who likes snacking on paperbacks in his free time. When she isn't thinking up new, exciting plots, Kinsley enjoys white wine, dark chocolate, and lots of coffee – not necessarily in that order. Constant acts of bravery and defeating the bad guys is hard work, after all.

Katekinsleyauthor.com

BROTHERHOOD PROTECTORS

ORIGINAL SERIES BY ELLE JAMES

Brotherhood Protectors Series

Hot SEAL Hawaiian Nights (SEALs in Paradise)

ABOUT ELLE JAMES

ELLE JAMES also writing as MYLA JACKSON is a *New York Times* and *USA Today* Bestselling author of books including cowboys, intrigues and paranormal adventures that keep her readers on the edges of their seats. With over eighty works in a variety of sub-genres and lengths she has published with Harlequin, Samhain, Ellora's Cave, Kensington, Cleis Press, and Avon. When she's not at her computer, she's traveling, snow skiing, boating, or riding her ATV, dreaming up new stories. Learn more about Elle James at www.elle-james.com

Website | Facebook | Twitter | GoodReads | Newsletter | BookBub | Amazon

Follow Elle!
www.ellejames.com
ellejames@ellejames.com